in a Bag

Written by Roderick Hunt
Illustrated by Nick Schon,
based on the original characters
created by Roderick Hunt and Alex Brychta

OXFORD
UNIVERSITY PRESS

Read these words

in	cat
bag	tin
hat	had
tub	tap

Wilf had a cat.

He put a hat on the cat.

Wilf had a bag.

He put the cat in the bag.

tap, tap, tap

7

Wilf had a tub.

He put the bag in the tub.

tap, tap, tap

9

Wilf had a tin.

He put the tub in the tin.

tap, tap, tap

11

Wilf had the cat in his hat.

Talk about the story

What did Wilf put on the cat?

Why was Wilf dressed up?

How did the cat get on top of Wilf's head?

What magic trick would you like to do?

Missing letters

Choose the letter to make the word.

ct

W___lf

t___n

h___t

What's in the picture?

Match the words to things you can find in the picture.
Point to the ones you can find.

Wilf   tub   bag

tin   cat   hat

It

Written by Roderick Hunt
Illustrated by Nick Schon,
based on the original characters
created by Roderick Hunt and Alex Brychta

OXFORD
UNIVERSITY PRESS

Read these words

him   Mum

hit   rug

fit   but

did   mud

Chip put on the cap.

He was 'it'.

Mum ran and Kipper ran.
Mum got on the box.

Kipper got on the rug.

Biff ran.

She got on the box.

Dad ran, but Chip got him.

Dad put on the cap.
It did not fit.

24

Bam! Dad ran into Floppy.

Dad hit the mud.

Talk about the story

Missing letters

Choose the letter to make the word.

b_x

r_g

m_d

l_g

What's in the picture?

Match the words to things you can find in the picture.

Point to the ones you can find.

box   on   dog   mud

Mum   log   rug   run

Word search

How many words can you find with *a, o, i* or *u* in them?
Can you write them down?

c	a	t	i	n
o	r	u	g	u
p	i	l	o	g
b	o	x	i	p
t	a	h	i	m